The Lichfield Jigsaw Murders

The Lichfield Jigsaw Murders
The Lichfield Writers

ISBN-13: 978-1-912605-56-9
ISBN-10: 1-91-260556-2
Published by j-views Publishing, 2018

www.j-views.biz
j-views Publishing, 26 Lombard Street, Lichfield, UK, WS13 6DR

Introduction and Acknowledgements

WE STARTED THIS as a light-hearted exercise. Little did we know how difficult it would be for us jointly to commit a murder in Lichfield and then solve it, without giving too much away to the readers before the time was right.

We were lucky that Jim and Hugh have experience in these matters (writing about murders, that is, not committing them) and were able to fit the different parts of the jigsaw together to make a whole picture.

Thank you also to our newest member, Kent Parson, who read through the almost-finished product and suggested some changes to improve the story that you now hold in your hands.

The cover image is a painting by David Brown, who served in the West Bromwich and Lichfield City Police Forces for several years during the 1960s and early 1970s before becoming a social worker, and whose work has been featured on the covers of a number of Jim's books. Thank you, David.

Lastly, we would like to remember our oldest member, Una Adams, who passed away in the summer of 2018, and whose work is featured in our first collection of writing, *Reflections*. She is remembered and missed.

Cathy Dobbs
(Founder of Lichfield Writers)
Lichfield, December 2018

The Lichfield Jigsaw Murders

by
The Lichfield Writers

j-views Publishing, Lichfield, England

Thursday 1 March 2018
Day 1 of the investigation

DETECTIVE INSPECTOR JEAN MASON slammed the car door, and going to the boot, took out a pair of green wellingtons and slipped them on. At five foot eight she was tall and slim and usually dressed in well-fitting clothes, but today she looked like the Michelin Man's wife, dressed in a long skirt, two jumpers, a body warmer and a padded overcoat.

It was the first of March, officially almost spring, but the day was bitterly cold. The temperature gauge in her car said −6C but the cold north-easterly wind made it feel like minus 14. *Something else to thank Mr Putin for*, she thought as she stood up, locked the car and walked carefully up the embankment to the path surrounding Stowe Pool. Lichfield had been largely untouched by 'The Beast from the East' and there was barely any snow on the grass, but Mason had no intention of giving the boys a story to tell and embellish about how the Boss had gone arse over tip on the icy embankment.

✳

THE PATHOLOGIST HAD ALREADY ARRIVED, and a yellow and white tent had been erected over the path and

2

embankment where the body had been found by an early morning dog walker. Forensics were combing the embankment and the banks of the Pool for clues. They'd be there until it got dark, and Mason was glad that it wasn't going to be her who would be outdoors all day.

The path was covered in black ice, and Mason walked with great care to where Sergeant Kramer, a 22-year veteran of the service with a shaved head, a well-developed beer belly, and a scalpel-sharp mind, was waiting for her. 'What have we got, Michael?' she asked, brushing a lock of blonde hair behind her ear.

'A dead woman. Mid to late twenties by the look of her. She's been strangled and had her head smashed into the path a few times before being rolled down the embankment. Her blood – well, probably hers – is still visible on the path, Boss.'

'Right, let's see her.'

Kramer stood aside and Mason entered the tent. The pathologist was Dr Phillip McGuire, a cheerful Irishman with a full grey beard, and dyed black hair who usually hummed when examining a body, but was now silent. 'What's the story, Phillip?'

'And good morning to you too, Jean. How are you?'

'I'm good, and you?' she asked, a smile trying to form at her cold lips.

'You don't want to know about an old crock like me. Now if I was twenty years younger...'

This time the smile reached her eyes and she laid her hand on his shoulder before asking him again, 'What have we got, Phillip?'

'A young woman, aged between 25 and 29, who has been strangled. Looks like manual strangulation. The hyoid bone is broken. Post mortem injury to the back of her skull as well. Whoever killed her smashed her head into the path – several times.'

'Has she been molested in any way?'

'I don't think so, but I'll confirm that back at the mortuary as soon as they get her to Cannock. The PC who responded to the initial call found her handbag on the embankment. Forensics have it now. I asked them to hurry up and let you know its contents,' he said.

'Thanks. You're a mind reader. Okay, let me have a look.'

The pathologist bent down and lifted the white body sheet to reveal a face that Mason had seen only the previous day on the train from Birmingham to Lichfield.

❋

THE DEAD WOMAN and an older man had joined the train together at Sutton Coldfield, and sat down on the other side of the carriage. They had been talking quietly, both trying to keep their voices down, when suddenly the man, almost shouting, said 'You can't do that! I won't allow it!' Seemingly surprised at the sound of his own voice, the man blushed, and folding his arms, said no more until the train was approaching Lichfield City.

The young woman stood up and he stretched his legs out in front of her, preventing her from leaving her seat. 'Where are you going?'

'Where do you think?'

He withdrew his feet and she stepped past him and headed for the toilets behind the man. By the time the train stopped in Lichfield City she had not reappeared and the man looked back over his shoulder. The toilet door was still closed and read 'Occupied'. As the man fell back in his seat, Mason saw the woman step quietly from the toilet to the carriage, where she pushed the 'Open' button, stepped from the train and sprinted into the waiting room.

Well, good for her, thought Mason and suppressed a smile.

The end of the line was Lichfield Trent Valley, just a mile away from the City station. When the woman didn't reappear after the train had stopped, the man went to the toilet door and knocked hard on it. No answer. He noticed the 'Locked' sign was off, and pressed the toilet 'Open' button and watched the door slide open to reveal an empty cubicle. Rushing to the door, he pressed the door 'Open' button and jumped from the train, started to run, but stopped after ten yards, and walked quickly down the steps and out into the car park, where Mason saw him jump into a white Avenis taxi.

'You know her?' asked McGuire.

'No. But I saw her on the train yesterday with a middle-aged man who was insisting that he wouldn't allow her to do something?'

'Do what?'

'I've no idea. I'm going back to the station. Let me know when the autopsy is.'

'This afternoon at three sharp. Unless an outbreak of the plague erupts.'

✳

BACK AT THE STATION, Mason quickly briefed Chief Superintendent Clarke on the case. Lichfield wasn't known for serious violent crimes, and this one was out of the ordinary. Only the second murder in three years. The local press would be all over it before midday. Sitting at her desk, she brushed a lock of hair from her right eye and logged onto the system, then punched the speed dial on her phone to call Forensics.

The familiar voice of Bill Withers said, 'Morning, Jean.'

'Morning, Bill. Have you had time to do your stuff on the victim's handbag?' She didn't need to say which case. There was only one that mattered right now.

'Yes. I knew you'd want it ASAP. Jenny is just typing it up. She'll send it to you within the next ten minutes together with the photos.'

'Thanks, Bill, and thank Jenny for me too.' Hanging up, she started checking her emails but all she could think about was the body of a young woman who had been told yesterday that 'You can't do that. I won't allow it'. Her reverie was broken by a ping, which told her that a new message had arrived from Forensics. She smiled and clicked it open.

The report on the bag was short. The bag itself was from Primark, but the pale blue purse with a Scottie dog wearing a tartan scarf was from Debenham's. It contained £52.39 and a receipt for coffee at the Boswell Bites café, dated February 28, and timed at 5:18. A credit and a debit card, both issued by a high street bank, both in the name of Nicola Toomey, and a typed letter from a Doctor Lunham of Lichfield.

She clicked on the email attachments and saw that the letter confirmed an appointment at his surgery at seven the previous evening, 28 February. The reason for attendance was not specified, but did mention that she would be required to settle her bill following the procedure. The address of the surgery was near Stowe Pool *Odd*, thought Mason, *Nicola Toomey's address wasn't on the letter*.

Other attachments included a photo of Nicola Toomey with her arm around a handsome young man who looked as if he'd just left university and a printout of an email from someone, presumably her boss at Randell and Hopkins, Solicitors, authorising a day's leave today – the 1st of March. There was an address with a telephone number below the signature on the email. No phone had been discovered in the bag or on the body. *Had the killer taken it?* she asked herself.

The report concluded that, at least on a preliminary showing, there was only one set of prints on the bag and the contents that had been tested so far, and these could probably be assumed to be the victim's. There were no blood splatters, which would be consistent with the wounds inflicted and the position of the bag relative to the body, some 150cm away to the victim's right.

Picking up the phone, Mason asked the switchboard to put her through to the writer of the email, a Mr Bright of Randell and Hopkins, Newhall Street, Birmingham. Ten minutes later she had the home address of the mother, Mary Toomey, as the nominated next of kin. Mason picked up her car keys and asked the desk sergeant if there was a WPC available who could accompany her on a death notification and headed out to the compound to wait for WPC Clayton, who joined her five minutes later.

'Where to, Boss?'

Mason gave her an address in Newtown, Birmingham, where they would deliver the worst possible news that any parent can ever receive.

✳

As WPC CLAYTON expertly wove the car through the heavy Birmingham traffic, Mason took advantage of the fact that for once she wasn't driving, and used the time to think and plan ahead. Before leaving the station, she'd given a description of the man she'd seen with Nicola the day before on the train, instructed Sergeant Kramer to set up an incident room, gulped down a mug of strong black coffee and devoured an old chocolate bar she'd found lurking at the bottom of her handbag. She'd also asked Kramer to track down the driver of the Toyota Avensis taxi which had taken the man to God knows where – and Mason definitely wanted to know where.

Bloody hell, even when she went shopping on her day off it resulted in work. Talk about being in the wrong place! she thought.

'We're here.' WPC Clayton's voice penetrated Mason's thoughts.

'Here' proved to be a desolate jumble of concrete tower blocks and maisonettes made even uglier, if that were possible, by more recent garish renovations of cheap white plastic-framed double glazing and orange cladding. Mrs Mary Toomey, the deceased's mother, lived at 62, Wellington Tower. Advising the next of kin was, in Mason's opinion, the worst part of her job, although time spent in the mortuary came a very close second.

Mary Toomey opened the door and Mason found herself looking down at a small woman who had probably once been pretty but now had lost her looks. She looked past Mason and saw Clayton's police uniform, 'What do you want? I ain't done nothing wrong,' she said her speech suspiciously slurred even at eleven in the morning.

'May we come in, Mrs Toomey? We have some bad news for you, I'm afraid.'

'No. I ain't cleaned up the place yet,' she said and laughed at her own witticism. The folds of fat around her neck and stomach moved up and down and Mason was conscious of the smell of cider and something stronger radiating from the woman.

Mason doubted that the overweight woman in front of her was capable of understanding the news she was about to deliver, but stepping forward said, 'The news I have for you is better said in private,' and pushed past the woman into the hall. WPC Clayton followed her.

'Well you're in now, ain't you? So tell me what's so important that you bullied your way past a sick old woman.'

'I'm sorry to inform you, Mrs Toomey, but your daughter Nicola was found dead in Lichfield this morning. We are treating her death as a case of murder, I'm afraid.'

What little colour was in Mrs Toomey's face drained away and she staggered backwards and slid down the wall. Sitting on the dirty carpet, head in her hands, the big woman's full figure disintegrated into a mound of anguished sobbing from which the only intelligible words to emerge were 'My poor baby'. After a few minutes of this, the two police officers helped the woman to struggle to her feet and stagger into the sitting room, where in preference to a cup of tea she poured herself a large glass of gin before adding a dash of orange squash. Gradually the alcohol produced a calmer state. Mason, whilst apologising for having to ask intrusive questions, gently began the process of learning more about Nicola's life.

'No. Nicola don't live here any longer. She's got her own flat but she spends a lot of time at her boyfriend's. That's where I thought she were last night. What were she doing in Lichfield?'

'We don't know yet. When did she leave home?'

'As soon as she had enough to buy herself a flat. She used to come back and see me regular like, but not so much in the last four months. She don't get on with David. He's my boyfriend.' she said with a trace of pride. 'We've been together for the past 18 months.'

When quizzed further, she explained, 'Nicola dain't like the fact that David was only twenty-eight. She thought he was too young for me and she dain't like his mates neither. 'Mindless layabouts' is what she called them', she sniffed.

'Can I ask about Nicola's father?' Mason asked.

'That crock of Irish shit. A right bastard. He's nothing but a thug who ain't afraid to use bully-boy tactics to get his own way.' Her response was delivered with real venom. 'And no, I ain't seen the fucker in years and I don't know where he lives either and I don't even care if he's still alive or not. Fucking bastard.'

'Do you have a picture of him?' asked Mason.

'No,' she replied, and then with an air of minor triumph said, 'I tore them all up and set fire to them the week he walked out that door.'

'Do you know if Nicola kept in touch with him?' asked Mason.

'Not as far as I know, but if she did, she wouldn't have told me, but I'm pretty sure that he sometimes wrote to her and called her at work.'

After obtaining photos and contact details for John Woodhead, Nicola's boyfriend, and David Wrekin, the mother's friend, and their addresses, Mason called the local police at Summer Lane and asked if they could supply a Liaison Officer to sit with Mrs Toomey for the rest of the day.

While Mason and WPC Clayton waited for the liaison to arrive they inspected Nicola's old bedroom. Unlike the rest of the house, the room was immaculate except for a layer of dust. Unfortunately, there was nothing left in the room that seemed to relate to her murder, and both officers were glad when they heard the bell ring and they were able to escape into the icy cold fresh air.

※

ON THE DRIVE BACK TO LICHFIELD, Mason wondered what David Wrekin was like. In twenty years with the police she had seen how certain women always seemed attracted to the worst possible men. Was it possible that Wrekin was just a younger version of Mrs Toomey's first husband? A bully and a thug. If so had he tried it on with Nicola? Was that the reason she'd left home?'

As she neared Lichfield she started to think about Dr Lunham. It seemed an odd time for an appointment. What was its purpose? Why have it so late in the day? Nicola's appointment had been for seven the previous evening, so even if all of this was totally innocent, the doctor may well have been the last person to see Nicola alive. Making her mind up she told Clayton to drive to St Chad's Church near Stowe Pool and park just yards away from Dr Lunham's clinic.

Lunham struck Mason as being almost an extension of his fine Georgian premises; tall and elegant. His tailored suit and manicured fingernails created a polished, neat exterior. He confirmed that Nicola Toomey had been scheduled to undergo an abortion the previous day but had failed to keep the appointment. He and his nurse had waited until eight o'clock before switching off the lights and locking up.

'Is it that usual, patients failing to show up?' she asked.

'No, but it's very unusual to have a total no-show on the day itself. Most cancellations occur the day before. That's why we insist on a minimum fifty per cent of the total fee as a deposit. I was surprised in this case, because Miss Toomey at the initial consultation had appeared calm and determined to have the procedure. She even declined to make use of our counselling service.'

'Did she give you any reason as to why she wanted the termination?'

'No, and I didn't ask.'

Mason couldn't help raising an eyebrow on discovering that in addition to the £95 initial consultation fee, Nicola had also paid the deposit of £750 in cash. Where, she wondered, had this money come from? And if Nicola had intended to have the abortion, where was the balance of £750 in cash? It hadn't been in her handbag.

'So you weren't alone here last night?'

'Good Lord, no. My nurse was here. We waited until eight, then she left, then I locked up and drove home.' Lunham stopped talking for a moment, and added, 'There was something that struck me as odd. As I was leaving I noticed a man standing across the road, a short distance away from the bottom of the drive. I remember thinking I wouldn't want to be hanging around on such a cold night.'

Mason probed further and Lunham told her that the man had appeared to be alone and no, he wouldn't describe him as being well-built. Quite the opposite, in fact.

❋

WHEN MASON PARKED outside the mortuary in Cannock, the weather had turned bitter. The day had grown colder as it advanced, and the cold wind sought out any skin that wasn't covered and quickly turned it blue with cold. Five minutes later she entered the mortuary to be greeted by Dr McGuire.

'Now don't you look a vision of loveliness?' he smirked as she walked in.

'Cameron Diaz would struggle to look good in this,' Mason retorted, referring to the drab green garment she was shrouded in. 'Just give me the preliminaries, Phillip, and I'll get out of your way.'

'As I thought earlier, manual strangulation leading to asphyxiation seems to have been the cause of death, but just to make sure, the job was done thoroughly. The perp pounded her head onto the tarmac path, causing several wounds to the back of the head. Fractured occipital and parietal. If you want my view, it's that he or she was pretty wound-up, frenzied even. Vicious injuries.'

'Any signs of resistance?'

'Not much. It looks like she was taken by surprise. As she was wearing gloves, there seems to be nothing useful under her fingernails, so that's one CSI clue we can't use. I might have more for you later. Also, you might be interested to know that the young lady was 15 weeks pregnant. As to the time of death, I would estimate between eight and midnight, although, given that last night's temperatures dropped to around minus fifteen I can't be certain. It's really just an educated guess. Don't rely on it. Other than that you see before you a fine specimen of a female in her mid- to late twenties, just a little bit strangled, and with a mildly crushed skull.'

Mason assumed that a dark sense of humour was a prerequisite for becoming a pathologist. Or maybe it was part of the curriculum at medical school.

Back in the car, Mason devoted a few moments to sorting the gathered information into a semblance of order in her mind. Mrs. Toomey's alibi for yesterday evening of bingo followed by drinks with the girls at the White Hart until eleven needed to be checked. She urgently needed to interview both David Wrekin and Nicola's boyfriend, John Woodhead, whose name and address Mary Toomey had promised to provide, and tomorrow would have to be spent at Nicola's employers, Randell & Hopkins, Solicitors.

Meanwhile, now she had absolute confirmation, she would have to break the news of the pregnancy and Nicola's intentions. She wondered who, if anyone, would find the news distressing. Her phone's chirpy ringtone roused her from her reverie.

'Mason, I want you at Stowe Pool as soon as possible,' bellowed the familiar voice of Chief Superintendent Clarke. 'The press are sniffing around asking questions, and I need you to head them off before local residents start getting upset.'

Mason couldn't help sighing. This was the part of the job she could do without. No matter how much information you gave the press, they always wanted more. It took patience to explain to a news-hungry journalist what had happened, as you had to pick your words carefully. Say one wrong word, or give out too much information, and the results could be catastrophic.

'Yes, Sir, I'm on it,' she hung up, gave Clayton the instruction to head back to Stowe Pool and cursed under her breath, 'Fuck.'

Before leaving the station she'd checked what had already gone out on social media – gone were the days when the press didn't find out anything until a statement had been released by the police. Now the police sent out tweets as soon as an incident occurred, and with the area around Stowe Pool closed, regular updates would be expected. You would have thought that newspaper editors would have loved this – but they hated it. It grated on them that the police were now at the forefront of breaking news, not the hacks.

With the car parked near St. Chad's church, she saw the TV van nearby, and knew she would have to smarten herself up a bit. Taking a comb and a lipstick from her bag, she started to tidy up. A few quick swipes through her shoulder-length hair and a touch of lipstick, and she felt ready for the cameras. Walking up to the police tape she saw well-known TV reporter Heather Wright flicking a piece of imaginary fluff off her shoulder before she prepared to do her piece in front of the camera. As Mason stopped to talk to one of the police officers on duty she heard the click-click of a photographer getting shots of her, and turned around to see local freelancer Bob Jones snapping away.

'You're looking good, Detective Inspector Mason,' he said, peering up from behind his lens. 'You lost a bit of weight?'

'What a charmer you are – and you wonder why you're still single,' Mason laughed as she walked over to the photographer, whom she'd known since she'd started in the police force more than 20 years ago. 'So, c'mon, Bob – give me the gossip. What do you know?'

'Probably more than you think – the reporter I'm working with today had a tip-off from the deceased's mother. I'm presuming she called all the regional press, because Dave with the camera and Heather over there are heading to her house after this to do a tribute piece.'

Mason clenched her teeth. Why did everyone have to be so fame-hungry these days? Mary Toomey must have called all the press even before she'd reached the A38 back to Lichfield.

'Detective Inspector Mason! Cooee!' Heather Wright

called out as she tottered over the grass in her four-inch stilettos. 'It would be wonderful if you could join me for an interview – your Superintendent said on the phone it wouldn't be a problem.'

Pasting a smile on her face, Mason nodded her agreement and went over to the cameraman, who wanted the interview to take place with the backdrop of the pool and the three spires of Lichfield Cathedral behind them. Mason had done a number of interviews like this before and trotted out the usual lines, such as, 'We are following all lines of enquiry' and 'Our team are working around the clock to find out who's responsible for this despicable crime.'

As the piece drew to a close, Heather turned to the camera, and Mason spotted a young man watching from the edge of the cordoned-off area, who even at a distance of thirty metres seemed agitated and vaguely familiar. When he realised she had noticed him he turned and walked away – a little too quickly for Mason's liking. Walking over to the nearest duty officer, she gave him a quick description, asking him to radio it out to all officers and she set off in the direction the youth had taken.

He'd been walking in the direction of the Cathedral, and her gut instinct told her he had carried ahead on to Dam Street. Her instinct had been right, as she saw the slim young man turn left and head into town. Following not too far behind, she winced when she saw him turn, and with wild eyes clock that he was being followed. It was then that she recognised how she knew his face – it was the young man from the photo in Nicola Toomey's handbag.

His pace quickened and suddenly he was running at full pelt through the Market Square. Mason was thankful that she had never succumbed to pressure to look glamorous at work, as her sensible flat brogues and loose skirt meant she could still sprint when needed. Spotting two officers outside the café in the square she shouted 'Go, go, go!' pointing in the direction of the youth, and they set off at speed, one talking into his radio as he ran, while the other sprinted ahead, arms and legs pumping. As she rounded the corner by the bank, she saw the officer had caught up with the young man and had him pressed up again the window of one of the estate agents on Bore Street.

As Mason caught her breath she heard him say his name – John Woodhead. So this really was Nicola's boyfriend.

'You're John Woodhead, aren't you? Nicola Toomey's boyfriend.' He nodded. 'Why did you run?' she demanded walking over to him.

'I know you think it was me, I know it.' The young lad had tears in his eyes. 'But it wasn't, I swear I would never have hurt Nicola, not with her carrying my baby.'

The familiar click-click of the photographer made Mason turn – of course, Bob had followed, he knew her too well.

'Stop it, Bob,' she said. 'This isn't a press conference – it's an interview. Respect this young man's privacy, if you would. I'll be seriously annoyed if I see any pictures of this anywhere.'

Bob sighed.

'Let's go back to the station – we can talk about it there,' Mason said to Woodhead as an officer radioed for a car to come and pick them up.

Back at the station, Woodhead was taken straight to an interview room and, after grabbing cups of tea for them both, Mason joined him. 'So how did you learn of Nicola's death?'

'Facebook. That fat cow of a mother posted the news this morning.'

'When did you last see Nicola?'

'She met me in that burger place in the Market Square – Boswell Bites, or whatever it's called – before her appointment at the clinic. You know about the clinic and all that?' Mason nodded in confirmation. 'I begged her not to go through with the termination, but she wouldn't listen to me,' John pleaded. 'She said I was too young to be a father, but I'm only two years younger than her. I was so angry with that I threw my fries at her and stormed out. That's the last time I saw her, I promise.'

'What did you do after that?'

'I started to go back home to Erdington, but I thought "I can't let her do it – it's my baby as well". So I went to the clinic and waited outside for her, but she never showed up. I waited until the clinic closed and saw the doctor locking up and it made me think she may have changed her mind. So I went home.

'I know she was only six or seven weeks pregnant. She said that the earlier you do it the easier the termination, but I just wanted her to wait – until we had a better idea of what we both wanted to do.'

'Six weeks pregnant?' questioned Mason, knowing that on examination the pathologist had judged the foetus to be around fifteen weeks.

'Yes, I'd been away on a four-month trip to America for work – part of my training. When I got back home we were so pleased to see each other again that we got – careless.

'I never thought...,' he sobbed. 'I never thought that just a few weeks later she would be dead,' He put his head in his hands and his body shook with tears.

She looked at the young man with a mixture of empathy and annoyance. It wasn't worth carrying on the interview now. She'd continue later. John Woodhead wasn't going to go anywhere. Being the last person to see Nicola alive was enough to hold him overnight. Besides, it was unlikely that he could answer the question that Mason desperately wanted answering: if John wasn't the father – who was?

❊

AFTER A VERY LATE LUNCH, Mason called a meeting of the entire team to discuss the case. Sergeant John Kramer had set up the incident board around which the team of six now sat.

Standing up, Mason said, 'Okay. For most of you a murder case is new ground. We don't get many of them in Lichfield. But I've been involved in a fair few and the thing that causes the worst problems is lack of communication. A small seemingly unimportant piece of information is known to just one person. But because it seems unimportant, so insignificant, they don't pass it on to anyone. When in truth it's the piece, which when added to the other information we have reveals the killer or their motive. It's a jigsaw puzzle where one piece is enough to complete the picture, and if that piece gets swept under the carpet, we can't finish the job. I don't want that happening to us. So we'll have an all-hands briefing every day, about this time, for as long as the investigation goes on and we haven't identified the killer.

'So what do we need to find out?' Mason asked and picked up a black marker pen and started to write on the white-board. 'Firstly, we need to identify the man on the train who said, 'I won't allow it'. Now, from what Mrs Toomey has told us, it could be her ex-husband. So, John, can you look into that, please. Start with the CCTV at the station and see if you can get a good picture of the man that we can show Mrs Toomey.'

'I'm already on it, Boss, but from a different angle. I've looked at the CCTV and identified that the taxi the man used is part of the Three Aces fleet and the driver should know where his fare was dropped off. I'm due to see him to-morrow morning – he's off today visiting relatives in Luton.'

'Good work,' said Mason. 'Let me know what you find out, but keep with the CCTV footage as well. Secondly,' and another line appeared on the whiteboard, 'the autop-sy reveals that that Nicola was fifteen weeks pregnant. However, her boyfriend, who has been in America on a training course for four months and has only recently re-turned thinks that the baby was his.'

'Was he off sick the day his sex education class talked about pregnancy and contraception or is he just thick?' asked WPC Clayton.

'I don't think he's thick. He was led to believe that it was his child. But as you clearly have an interest in all things medical,' she smiled, 'why don't you take on board checking where Mr Woodhead was and what he was doing during his four months in the States.'

Clayton held up her hand again and asked, 'Why didn't Nicola arrange a discreet abortion as soon as she had realised her situation? It would have been a simple procedure at that time and her returning boyfriend need never have known that she had been unfaithful. Instead, she waited for him to return and told him that she was six weeks pregnant and that he was the father. Then, having told him that, she later says that she's going to terminate the pregnancy, justifying her intention with God knows what reason for her change of heart. And why Lichfield for the abortion? There are a lot more clinics in Birmingham and a lot cheaper too, than Lunham.'

Mason smiled again. 'All good questions. Now all you have to do is find the answers. You can start by speaking to Woodhead. He's in the cells as we speak. Then visit Dr Lunham. I'm pretty sure that he knows more then he's saying. And then a house-to-house to see if there's any other witnesses to our mysterious loiterer.

'Thirdly, why did Nicola leave home?' A large "3" went up on the board. 'Was it the mother's new boyfriend? Did he try it on with her? Was that the reason she finally left?' Turning towards an overweight woman in her fifties, Jean asked, 'Look into that for me, Carol.'

'Sure, Boss,' she replied with a smile.

'And fourthly, when I spoke to Dr Lunham he said that they charged 50% in advance of all procedures and 50% on completion of the procedure. Which in Nicola's case was two payments of £750. But she didn't have the operation yet there was no sign of the £750 in her handbag or about her body. I'll look into that – see if she had enough in her account to cover a card payment. Finally, Don and Sue to check out Nicola's movements between leaving the train and her death. See if they match what Woodhead has to say. And lastly,' she concluded with a final flourish on the whiteboard, 'where's the victim's bloody phone? No-one of that age goes around without one. It wasn't on the body, wasn't in her bag.'

'Perp threw it in the Pool?' suggested Clayton.

'Want to go swimming for it?' Mason asked. 'Seriously, that would be a possibility if the surface of the water wasn't frozen like it was when we saw it this morning.'

'But was it frozen yesterday evening?' Clayton persisted.

'Good point. We don't know, do we? Find out.'

'What will you be doing, Boss?' asked Kramer.

'Well, I'll be in the office for the next couple of hours, checking the money side of things, and a few other bits and pieces that I can do from behind a desk. But first thing tomorrow I'm off to see Randell & Hopkins, Solicitors, in Birmingham – Nicola's employers, for those of you who don't know. So I'll be in late in. Which will give you lot plenty of time to do what we've just discussed. Right?

There was a low murmur that sounded like 'Right, Boss'.

'I can't hear you,' she shouted, and this time the reply was loud enough to be heard in the cells below.

❋

Friday 2 March 2018
Day 2 of the Investigation

MASON AWOKE SUDDENLY with the sound of her alarm, shrill and demanding.

What day is it? she thought.

Reality kicked in. It's Friday. She began to regret taking the sleeping pills which dulled her early morning brain. Mason ran through her plans for the day. On a good day she always felt she was on top of her game but on a bad day she wondered if she was over the top. She wasn't sure what sort of day this was going to be, but years of experience told her that black coffee was always a good start. Throwing off the bedclothes, 'I can solve this.' she reassured herself, hoping the investigation was going to be straightforward.

She showered quickly and had a hurried breakfast. By the time she reached the car she was surprised how clear her thoughts were. *Maybe it will be a good day,* she thought.

❋

PULLING UP OUTSIDE THE EDWARDIAN BUILDING in Newhall Street, Mason was unsure what she could learn from Nicola's boss that was relevant to the case. Background, anyway. What sort of face had Nicola presented to the world? What did other people think of her?

A quick flash of her ID and Mason was whisked into an office by the receptionist, who then went to inform Mr Bright that the police had arrived. The office wasn't what Mason had been expecting – it was dingy and dated; the company appeared to be going through tough times. Mason turned as she heard the door open.

'Hello, sorry to keep you waiting, I'm Kenneth Bright,' said the elderly frail, rather unkempt man as he held out his hand. His grip was limp and his hand cold. 'I assume you are here to talk about the death of Nicola Toomey. What an unfortunate affair – now how can I help?' He gestured for her to sit at one of the desks and Mason took out her notebook and pen.

Bright spoke about how long Nicola had worked at the company, and what her role had involved. 'She was a good timekeeper and a hard worker – Nicola is a real loss to the practice.' His voice trembled as he spoke and Mason noticed the tear in his eye.

'You seem emotional – does it always upset you to lose a colleague?'

'She wasn't just a colleague, she was a dear friend and like a member of the family. Almost like the daughter I never had. The practice has gone through hard times. We have all supported each other, and she did more to keep spirits up then anyone.'

'Did you ever meet her boyfriend, John Woodhead?'

"Yes,' he said. 'Last Christmas he came in to pick Nicola up.'

'What did you make of him?'

'He seemed nice enough. A bit too full of himself for my liking, but Nicola seemed to like him.'

'Was he the boss in the relationship?'

'No, Nicola would never let him get away with anything like that.' He smiled. 'If you'd known her and seen them together, you wouldn't have asked that.'

'Did her mother's boyfriend, David Wrekin, ever visit

Nicola?'

'Not that I'm aware of. I don't recognise the name.'

'Did she tell you why she needed the day off yesterday?'

'I knew the reason. It was me that recommended Dr Lunham to her. It was the first time in four years that she had asked for a day's medical leave and I was happy to grant it.'

'And how did you know of Dr Lunham?'

''Every solicitor has a list of contacts that their clients might have reason to use. A colleague of mine, who left the practice under a bit of a cloud, had recommended him to me. I've never had any negative comments about Dr Lunham's services.'

'Would that cloud have anything to do with the difficulties you've been working through?'

'You're very bright, Inspector. I'm glad you are not investigating me. And yes, they were the start of our problems which are almost resolved now.'

'Was Nicola working here when these problems became apparent?'

'She was. In fact, she was working as the PA to this man when we found it necessary to– to ask him to stop working here.'

Mason asked for and received the name of the suspect colleague, though she felt this would turn out to be a blind alley.

Walking back to the car, Mason decided that Bright was not a suspect. He was too old and fragile to have committed such a vicious murder. Before she pulled away, her phone rang and she switched off the engine. 'Yes, what is it John?'

It was Sgt Kramer. 'Just a quickie, Boss. We've got the CCTV footage from the station cameras – but we are still waiting for the town centre's cameras. It should all be ready for the meeting this afternoon. Are you on your way back to the station?'

'Yes. Why?'

'I'm just going out to interview the cabbie.'

Mason didn't reply immediately. After a pause she said,

'No, John. You concentrate on getting what you can from the videos and I'll go and speak to the driver. What's his name?'

'Hamid.'

❋

MASON MADE HER WAY to the Three Aces office, located in the centre of the city. The dispatcher was busy taking bookings and nodded her head towards a tall, thin man with a Saddam Hussein moustache and wearing black slacks and a clean white shirt. He stood up immediately when he saw Mason walk into the office, looking nervous.

'This is Hamid,' the dispatcher said to Mason. 'He took the fare your people are asking about.'

'I never did anything, Miss,' Hamid said to her. 'I know there's been some trouble before, but this time, nothing. I swear it.'

'Don't worry, Hamid. You're not the problem this time.'

The taxi office was small and overcrowded with staff and drivers. Mason said that this was no place for a confidential interview, and the receptionist quickly showed Mason and Hamid into an empty room containing two chairs and a small wooden table.

'I think you've been told what this is about, so shall we just get on with it. You might be able to help us with some important information. You could be a very important witness.' Hamid sat up a little straighter, and a faint look of pride spread over his face. 'Can you tell me something about the fare you picked up at Trent Valley station on Wednesday evening at about half past five? Take your time.'

Hamid clasped his hands together and looked Mason straight in the eye.

'He was an odd one. Looked nervous. Didn't know where he wanted to go. Asked if any private medical clinics in Lichfield open this late.'

'What time was this?' enquired Mason.

'I looked at my log before meeting you today. About five thirty five. Don't know much about these clinics but remembered passenger asking to be taken to clinic six months ago. Don't forget. Can't help feeling for some passengers. Drove him round to the house near Stowe Pool'

'Did he get out?' asked Mason.

'No,' replied Hamid. 'Thought was strange. Then asked me take him to centre town. Dropped him off in Market Square. Watched him. Saw him go into pub.'

'And that was the last you saw of this man?'

'No. Later I saw him outside train station only one hour or so later. He was very drunk. Could not stand up.'

'Thank you, Hamid, you have been very helpful. Please let me know if you remember anything else.' She passed her card to the driver.

'Okay,' replied Hamid 'Sad murder. Lichfield such quiet place. Makes business bad.'

✳

BACK AT THE STATION, Mason poured herself a coffee, and picking up her sandwich that she'd bought from one of the stores in town after talking to Hamid, headed for the Incident Room and the team meeting she had scheduled for half past two. Checking her watch she saw that it was nearly four. Hell. Couldn't even keep her own appointments. Fine way to show leadership. The only person present when she arrived was John Kramer. Slumping into a chair Mason said, 'For goodness' sake, when are we going to get a clue to this murder?'

'It'll come. I can feel it in me water,' said Kramer. 'Remember the old saying slowly, slowly catchee monkey.'

'I thought it was softly, softly.'

'Well whatever it were, we'll catch this monkey.'

'Really?' Mason sighed. 'We've had no joy from the mother, we can rule Bright out and we can't find Nicola's phone. So, what are we looking at here?'

'Well, Boss, we need to check Woodhead's alibi that he left Lichfield on the 20.12 train to Birmingham – check that CCTV as well – and speak to the mother's boyfriend.'

'Get onto it, then. I put out an email to all nicks in

Staffordshire asking them to keep their eyes open for the mother's boyfriend and I also sent the picture of the man on the train. We should hear something soon. Get the rest of the team in here.'

As Kramer left the room, Mason sank into a chair and closed her eyes. An awful lot of nothing seemed to be happening. Not that she expected instant results, but it was frustrating that there was no one lead that stood out.

The remaining team members slowly wandered into the room and at ten past four, Mason opened her eyes stood up. 'Sorry for the delay. I got caught up. Right. Let's hear what you've found out since yesterday.'

Kramer stood up and cleared his throat. 'Well we've got CCTV from all the railway stations and it confirms what you said Boss. Nicola is seen boarding the train at Sutton with a man Mary Toomey tells us is probably Nicola's father, Mick. Sadly there's no CCTV available from the train, but platform footage from City shows Nicola hurrying off the train by herself, and then at Trent Valley we see the man we think is Mick Toomey leave the train and start off down the steps.'

'Good. Carol, what have you been able to discover about Nicola's movements in Lichfield between getting off the train and the time of her death?'

'Not a lot, Boss. We've got the CCTV footage and it shows Nicola and John together in the town centre, but this still had to be reviewed for closer examination. She was seen going into the Boswell Bites café with a young man at just gone six. He had a cheeseburger, chips and a cola, she had a black coffee. One of the burger flippers behind the counter remembered that they seemed to be having an argument, which ended with the boyfriend throwing his chips in her face and storming off. This was about quarter past. The flipper says she left about five minutes later and no one seems to have seen her since.'

'Okay. Keep digging. No one disappears in Lichfield for three or four hours without being seen by someone somewhere. I've spoken to the cabbie, Hamid,' said Mason. 'He

confirms that he took the man we have provisionally identified as Mr Toomey into the centre of town at a little after five thirty, and then took him to that Stowe Pool clinic
before taking him back to the centre at about six. What's
interesting is that Hamid then saw him again an hour later.
At that time he was pissed, almost legless, and out of his
mind at Lichfield City. We can guess he was heading back
to Sutton. For now we can assume that Michael Toomey is
out of the picture. But I still want to talk to him – he knows
things we don't. So, what else have we got?'

A PC put his head around the door of the incident room
to say, 'Sorry, Ma'am, but I thought you'd like to know that
Tipton nick has just rung us to say they have David Wrekin
in custody. GBH. They wanted to know if you wanted to
be interviewing him today.'

A broad smile spread across Mason's face, 'Damn' right
I do. Tell them I'll be there by six. Okay, some good news
at last. Clayton, have you had time to speak to Dr Lunham
yet?'

'Yes, Boss, I saw him while you were speaking to Hamid. I
got to say that I think he's dirty. Nothing recorded against,
but I'm certain he knows more about Nicola's murder then
he lets on.'

'Do you think he killed her?' asked Kramer.

'No. Not sure, but he's doing something. I'm sure of that
much.'

'And what evidence have you got?' asked Mason.

'None, Boss, but he's hiding something. I think it's to do
with his practice.'

'Why do you say that?' asked Mason.

'He doesn't have enough staff. For the size of his practice
he's only got one nurse plus an admin assistant/reception-
ist. I think he's either fiddling the books or fiddling with
some of his patients. He also didn't seem that clear on the
rules that deal with abortions. I took the trouble to look
some of them up.'

'Such as?' asked Mason.

Clayton opened her notebook, and referred to it as she

spoke. 'It's a legal requirment that at the initial appointment a doctor does a scan to confirm the age of the foetus and decide the suitability of the type of procedure. Twenty-four weeks is the limit.

'While Nicola might have genuinely misjudged the timing, at that first appointment Dr. Lunham ought to have discovered that her pregnancy was well advanced and made appropriate arrangements. Terminating a fifteen week pregnancy would require a more complex procedure with the possibility of an overnight stay. I don't think he has the facilities for overnight stays. Besides which, how much more would it cost? Private clinics typically charge from £400 to £2,000. The more advanced the pregnancy, the higher the cost and Nicola was at the extreme end. Nicola had not been invoiced for this. Why not? Some pieces of this story seem to be missing.'

Thinking back, Mason recalled the doctor referring to switching off the lights and locking up and leaving with his nurse. It was possible he had no other patients but there had been no mention of any other staff. Strange, because male gynaecologists and obstetricians often employed a second nurse, partly to assist in procedures but also to act as protection against any accusations of impropriety.

Clayton continued. 'Nor did he mention a chaperone or someone to accompany and support the patient on her journey home, which is recommended even after early weeks terminations, and the doctor seemed to have been waiting alone for Nicola, except for the nurse who was tidying up and locking up at the back, but had pointedly mentioned seeing a man loitering across the road.'

'And this conclusion that he's on the fiddle is built on your intuition?' asked Kramer, sarcastically.

Clayton blushed, but she wasn't willing to give up without an argument. 'No, it's based on my experience as a copper and before that I was an audit clerk in local government. I can spot a lying bastard a mile away, and he were lying about sommit.'

Kramer was about to respond, but Mason stepped in,

'Okay, Clayton. You and I will go and see him again in the morning. Get a DNA test done on the foetus. If they have to work overnight on it, that's tough, but I want an answer on that ASAP.'

'Will do, Boss.' Clayton wrote in her book, and pulled out her phone and started tapping.

'For now I want to find Mick Toomey,' Mason went on. 'I take it we released John Woodhead this morning?' The question was directed at Sergeant Kramer.

'Had to, Boss, as his solicitor said we had no hard evidence to hold him on.'

'Damn. But he's right. Carol, did you manage to find out when Nicola actually left home?'

'Yeah,' said Carol edging forward on her chair. 'The mother was out but I spoke to one of the neighbours. Nicola bought herself a flat about three years ago, but she used to always come home to spend one or two nights every week with her mum. But in late November last year the neighbour said she heard a right row going on.'

'Between Nicola and her mother?'

'Well, no. Mrs Toomey was out. The row which the neighbour swears turned into a fight was between Nicola and Wrekin as far as she could tell. It lasted about half an hour and ended with Nicola walking out with a black eye and her suitcase. The neighbour says Nicola never stays overnight now, and does everything she can to avoid Wrekin.'

'Got all that as a statement?' Carol nodded. 'Good stuff there.' Mason looked at her watch. It was now nearly half-past five and the roads between Lichfield and Tipton would be clogged with rush-hour traffic. 'Right, Michael, it's getting on. I'll ring Tipton and say we'll be there by eight tomorrow. I'll pick you up from yours at seven. Okay?'

'Fine by me, Boss.'

Returning to her office, Mason picked up the phone and rang Tipton nick to speak to the Custody Sergeant. After introducing herself she asked, 'Have you got enough on Wrekin to hold him until tomorrow?'

'Yeah we've already charged the little sod. GBH. He's due

in court Monday morning. '

'Great. I can't make tonight but will be there tomorrow morning – I'll try to make it by eight.'

'No problem, Ma'am.'

Saturday 3 March 2018
Day 3 of the investigation

Before leaving home, Mason put a call in to Rugeley Police Station and was told that Detective Sergeant Hughes was not on duty that day. After asking the desk Sergeant, who she'd trained with twenty years earlier, for Hughes' mobile number, she rang him and asked him for a favour before picking up Kramer and driving over to Tipton nick.

As they reached their destination, Mason's phone rang. 'Take it for me, Michael. I'm driving and I hate the sodding roads round here.' She passed her phone over and listened to Kramer's non-committal side of the conversation. Eventually he hung up.

'Well?'

'That was the DNA boys. They weren't happy about doing a rush job for you.'

'Surprise. Are they ever?'

'But they've got the father of Nicola's baby. He's a certain Damien Hunter.' He smiled.

She thought a bit, biting her lip as she negotiated a roundabout. 'We know Mr Damien Hunter, don't we?'

'Yep. He got three years a few months back for fraud and embezzlement, and he's still inside, as far as we know. His DNA's on file – it was part of the evidence that convicted him, remember – his saliva on the papers he'd taken.'

Mason did some calculations in her head. 'It fits with the timing. Just. Must have been when he was on bail awaiting trial. Bloody hell.'

'Didn't you say Nicola had been the PA to a dodgy lawyer?'

'I did. Hmmm.'

There was silence until they reached the Tipton police station.

Mason quite often had gut feelings about people, and the first time she saw David Wrekin was one of those occasions. He didn't even have to say anything – his eyes said it all as they lingered on certain parts of her body, making her flesh crawl.

When Mason and Kramer entered the room, Wrekin was sitting in a hard-backed chair behind the table, seemingly sulking. The look on his face changed to a leer as he saw Mason and Kramer enter the room.

'I'll have two sugars in my tea, darlin' – and while you're at it, piss off and get your boss? I don't talk to no cleaners,' sneered Wrekin.

Mason ostentatiously switched on the recording system and gave the date, time and name of all present in the room, stressing her rank, before asking, 'Mr Wrekin, can you please confirm your name and your relationship to the deceased Nicola Toomey.'

'No comment – you've got nothing on me on this one. I know my rights. I could just leave this room now and walk back to me cell.'

'Sit down and answer the questions – are you currently in a relationship with the deceased's mother?'

'I sleep with her, if that's what you're asking – but then I sleep with lots of women. Like I say to my mates – if it's got an ass, and a pair of tits then I'll shag it.'

'Does that include Nicola Toomey?'

'That stuck-up bitch!' David snarled, leaning forward menacingly in his chair. 'Thinking that she's better than us, working at that solicitors in Birmingham. She's just like every other woman – a cheap whore. Well, I showed her, didn't I?'

Mason's heart was pounding. 'Are you telling me you had sex with Nicola Toomey?'

'No comment,' smiled David, suddenly back to being cocky again. 'Now why don't you just trip off and get me that cup of tea?'

At that point there was a knock at the door and the Desk Sergeant entered the room. Mason signed off on the recording and said, 'What is it, Sergeant?'

'Sorry to disturb you, Ma'am but I've just received this message,' he said holding out a folded piece of paper.

Mason took it and her heart lurched in her chest as she read the message from WPC Clayton, which read, 'Nicola's father has just walked into the Station asking to speak to Detective Inspector Mason.'

Mason stood and walked out of the room, motioning to Kramer to follow her.

'No cup of tea then?' Wrekin shouted after her. She ignored him.

Outside the interview room Mason handed the note to Sergeant Kramer whose expression didn't change, and said, 'Michael, give the station a ring and tell them we'll be back with them before eleven. Then wait for Keith Hughes and bring him in when he arrives.'

'Sure, Boss.'

❈

BACK IN THE INTERVIEW ROOM, Mason switched on the recorder again and gave details of those present and the time.

When she'd finished Wrekin said, 'Left your boyfriend outside? Just in case you start to get overcome with lust and start ripping me clothes off?' he sneered.

'No, Mr Wrekin, he's making a phone call. He'll be along shortly.'

'You know, you've got a right posh voice. If the police don't work out for you could make a fortune on one of those sex lines. I could give you...'

Wrekin didn't have time to finish his sentence before the door opened and Kramer entered the room, with another man following him. Detective Sergeant Hughes wasn't a big man, he was massive. He weighed at least fifteen stone, and played as prop forward on the Staffordshire county police rugby team. His colleagues had been known to describe him as 'built like a brick shithouse', and he had a reputation among the local villains for being less than gentle in his handling of arrested suspects. At six foot six, or as near as damn it, with a massive chest and biceps the size of many a copper's thigh, he put the fear of God into anyone he was up against. A former Royal Marine, he was universally popular amongst his colleagues because they knew he would never let a mate down, regardless of the odds.

Following Mason's call and briefing on what she wanted, he'd dressed in a tight white T-shirt which set off his dark brown arms, and made him look even bigger than normal.

Wrekin's eyes were filled with fear. This black guy was a freak. 'Whatcha' bring this nignog Charles Atlas in for? Trying to scare me?

'You'll speak when you're spoken to and not otherwise.' Hughes's voice was soft and deep, but it carried undertones of unspeakable menace. 'Otherwise it won't be your clothes I'll start ripping off.' He looked down meaningfully at Wrekin's crotch.

'Fuck you,' said Wrekin, and before he knew it, he was sprawled painfully on the floor.

'Sorry about that. Me foot slipped,' said Hughes. 'Now pick up that chair, sit on it, and talk to the Inspector like a good boy.'

Wrekin slowly obeyed and sat down. He seemed to be in pain. Mason hadn't seen Hughes hit him, but somehow Wrekin's mouth was bleeding. 'I want a lawyer,' he said to Mason.

"I want, never gets'. Didn't your mother ever tell you that?' Kramer asked.

'He never had a mother,' said Hughes, conversationally.

'Shit like that slides out from the sewers on dark nights.'

Wrekin's face went black with rage. 'I'm not saying any-thing to you,' he said to Mason.

'I think you are going to,' said Hughes, and a second later, Wrekin was on the floor again.

'Get this fucking maniac out of here!' Wrekin shouted at Mason.

'See, I told you you'd start talking to her,' said Hughes. 'Now are you going to sit on that chair, or do you prefer the floor?'

Wrekin dragged himself to his feet, and warily perched himself on the chair.

'What was your relationship with Nicola Toomey?'

'I've already told you. She was a stuck-up bitch. Thought she was better than any of us. Well, stuck-up was the right word after I'd finished with her.'

'You're scum, you are,' Hughes hissed softly in his ear. Wrekin flinched but the blow never came.

'You know that she was pregnant when she died?'

'Nah. Not surprised, really.'

'And that the child was yours? DNA match,' she said, try-ing to keep a straight face. 'They've got yours on file from some time ago.'

'No way! I had the snip a few years back. Vasectomy. Don't want a whole load of little bastard Wrekins running around Brum, do we?'

'One little bastard Wrekin's quite enough, thank you,' said Hughes. He cuffed Wrekin, in an almost friendly way, across the ear.

'There's no way it could be mine! She lied to you! Just because she didn't want to and I was a bit rough about it. She lied to you,' he repeated.

'I don't think you were listening to the Inspector, Davy,' Hughes said in his quiet menacing voice. 'This is science, Davy-boy, not hearsay. Nicola is fucking dead and you killed her.'

'I never killed her. I may have been a bit rough with her like I said, but I never killed her. Honest.'

'You wouldn't know honest if it bit your dick off,' said Hughes.

'And by the way, you've just confessed to rape,' Mason added.

'Witnesses? You can't prove nowt.'

Mason nodded at the red light glowing on the recorder.

'Want to make a statement now?' Hughes whispered in Wrekin's ear. 'You might get off with only five years if you plead guilty on this one.'

✳

'Nice one, Inspector Mason,' said the Tipton Superintendent. 'We've been wanting to get this sod banged up for a long time.'

'Fruit of a poisoned tree, I'm afraid,' she said. 'I lied about him being the father of the unborn child.'

'Don't worry about it,' smiled the Superintendent. 'Two short planks are nothing compared to David Wrekin. He's probably forgotten about that part already. There's nothing about it in the statement, is there?'

'No.'

'Believe me, his lawyers come from the Poundland's bargain shelves. They might be able to get him off spitting on the grass, but that's their limit. The virgins of Tipton – both of them – can sleep easy in their beds, thanks to you.'

✳

After thanking Hughes for coming out on his rest day, Mason and Kramer drove back to Lichfield.

Before heading into Interview Room 1, Mason and Kramer spoke to Clayton about Toomey and watched him on the CCTV for five minutes. She recognized him immediately as the man she had seen on the train with Nicola. The man was still wearing the same clothes as he'd worn on Thursday, except he'd fallen down a few times and his suit and overcoat were dirty.

'What's he want to talk to you for, Boss?' asked Clayton. 'Do you think he's come to confess?'

'To a murder he couldn't have committed? He was in Sutton nick when it happened. They picked him up off the train for D&D.'

'So what's he coming to us for, then?'

'We're about to find that out. He asked them in Sutton who was in charge here, and they gave him my name. Probably just wants a shoulder to cry on drunkenly.'

Entering the interview room Mr Toomey stood up, and said, 'Thank you for seeing me,' and held out his hand. Both Mason and Clayton shook his hand. He seemed sober enough, as far as she could tell.

'I'm terribly sorry about your daughter, Mr Toomey,' Mason said. She could afford to establish some sort of emotional bond, since she knew he was innocent, at least of the murder. 'We'll find the person who did it, trust me.'

'I think you've found him already, but you just don't have enough pieces of the jigsaw to see the whole picture. I might be able to help you.'

Mason started. The image of the jigsaw was one she'd used herself to describe the case. She asked Toomey if he'd prefer tea or coffee, and left Clayton to arrange this.

As the door closed Toomey said, 'I'm Mick, by the way.'

'Fine. Now, what have you got for me, Mick? Just so you know, we're recording this, so you won't see me taking a lot of notes. Any objections?'

He shook his head. 'No. I reckon that's okay by me.' He studied her curiously. 'Weren't you on the train to Lichfield, the day that...?'

'Yes, I was. I noticed you.'

'Couldn't very well miss me, could you? Made a right bloody fool of meself, didn't I? So would you, if you'd been in my place.'

She waited. Saying nothing was often the best way to get the information she needed. The coffee arrived, and she sat in silence while he spooned sugar into his cup and stirred it, his eyes not meeting hers.

'First off, I made a right idiot of myself afterwards with that vodka, didn't I?'

'Well, the taxi driver said you looked the worse for wear when he saw you later on outside the station.'

'I'll tell you about that. I was an alkie. A right piss-artist. You've met Nicola's mum?' Mason nodded. 'Well, I was as bad then as she is now. Worse, in fact. And her and me, we fought all the time. Well, that's no life. Not fair on me, not fair on her, not fair on little Nickie. So I moved out, but kept in touch with my little girl. And then I dried out.' He paused. 'I didn't touch a drop for over ten years, but the other day, well...' His voice tailed off.

'You didn't want Nicola to do something,' Mason suggested gently. 'And she was determined to do it.'

'I didn't want her to kill what was inside her, even if it was that bastard's.'

'Who are we talking about?'

'David fucking Wrekin, that's who, pardon my French. You know who I'm talking about, don't you?'

'We've talked to him.'

'Then you know what kind of a little shit he is. Nickie was pregnant with his baby. That's what she told me.'

Mason didn't respond. The DNA tests had confirmed the father wasn't David Wrekin's. 'She and David Wrekin were...?'

'It was rape, the way she told it to me. Have you seen that bastard's record?' She shook her head. 'It's a mile long. Sexual assault, indecent behaviour, the whole bloody shopping list short of actual rape. I guess they were all too scared of him to come forward. Plus what I suppose you'd call the usual – theft, some GBH, dealing, whatever. He's a vicious bastard, that one.'

'It sort of makes sense,' she said half to herself. 'But part of it doesn't.'

'What?'

'The post-mortem told us her pregnancy was too advanced to be her boyfriend's.' Mick Toomey snorted. 'But the DNA said it was someone else's.' Toomey looked at her questioningly.

'It doesn't matter who. Now about the doctor. Doctor

Lunham, who she was going to see.'

'She never told me a name. Just she was going to see someone to take care of things.' He seemed lost in thought for a moment. 'DNA is pretty final proof, isn't it?'

'Yes. Except when it goes wrong. Samples get mixed up, they get contaminated by other samples or by the lab techs, and DNA's not unique, you know. Just odds of a few million to one that your DNA and mine, for example, are the same.'

'Oh.' A brief silence. 'Anyway, she gave me the slip at Lichfield City.'

She smiled. 'I saw that.'

'I was bloody livid. When we got to Trent Valley, I saw that the train wasn't going back for another fifteen minutes, so I raced down the steps and got a taxi back into the city. I looked around, but I had no idea where she had got to. I was still mad, and I wanted to strangle David Wrekin for what he'd done to my little girl. Strangle him slowly.'

'I can understand how you felt.'

'I hadn't touched the stuff for ten years, like I said, but I went into one of the pubs in the centre, then got myself a bottle of vodka and headed back on the train from City. I must have drunk half the bottle before I went to the station and the rest waiting for the train. I don't remember much after that. They hauled me off at Sutton for drunk and disorderly, and kept me for observation for a day or so. Then I found out about Nickie from the *Express & Star*. Hadn't seen anything until then.' He put his head in his hands. 'If only I'd been with her. Hadn't yelled at her the way I did.'

Mason felt a stab of sympathy for the man sitting before her, now weeping. 'Not your doing. Here's a tissue,' she said, pushing the box towards him.

'Thanks. You must reckon I'm soft in the head,' he said, with a wry smile.

'Not at all. You're a loving father who only wanted the best for his little girl.'

Silence. Then, 'Thank you.'

'What do you make of John, Nicola's boyfriend, by the

way?'

'He's okay, I guess. Bit young for Nicola, really. Bit of a kid.'

She remembered him crying when she had first talked to him by Stowe Pool, and nodded.

'Got a shocking temper on him, mind,' Toomey went on.

'Oh, Violent?'

'He could be.'

'Towards Nicola?'

'Nah. If he'd tried any of that, he knew what was coming to him. I wouldn't let Nicola put up with that kind of shit. But he and Nickie and me was sat in a pub one night. They were drinking something – gin and tonic if I remember right, and I was on the soft stuff – lemonade, while we were waiting for a table for our meal. Then some joker started to make wisecracks about the T-shirt John was wearing. Something about Jeremy Corbyn. Well, his face went white, but it was an angry kind of white. I've never seen anyone like that before. He started shaking, and he was ready to kill. I could see it in his eyes.'

'And?'

'I went over to the joker and told him to get out fast. Said John had been with the Marines, despite what he looked like. I reckon I said it right, because he got up and went out into the garden straight off.'

'And John?'

'He was right as rain in a few seconds, it seemed like. Carried on as if nothing had happened. But it scared me, the way he changed like that. Normal to maniac and normal again, all inside a couple of minutes.'

'Listen, you told me at the start of our conversation that we might have already found the murderer, but we don't know who he is. What do you mean by that?'

'Just a feeling. Nickie wouldn't ever let anyone near her unless she knew them. Listen, there was nothing in the papers about her being raped or anything.'

'That's right. There was no evidence of anything like that.'

'And was anything taken from her bag or out of her

pockets?'

She shook her head. 'Difficult to say, but there was over fifty pounds in cash in her bag, and her cards were all there. I guess nothing was taken, but there should have been £750 pounds to pay the doctor if it was going to be cash, and there wasn't. And she'd drawn that amount out of the bank that morning.'

'Doesn't that mean that it was someone she knew?'

'It might,' she admitted.

'And have you been rounding up all the tramps and rough sleepers and the ones who cause fights outside the pubs at night round here and asking them where they were?'

'No.'

He sat back triumphantly. 'Then I'm right. You have been talking to Nicola's murderer. You just don't know it yet.'

There wasn't much more to say. He drank his tea and ate three chocolate digestive biscuits before he left. 'Thanks for listening.'

'Thank you for coming to see me.'

They shook hands and she went back to her desk.

❋

CHECKING HER COMPUTER, Mason Googled 'CloudCrossing Networks,' found the number and made her call to Woodhead's employers. The phone was answered by a pre-recorded message, 'CloudCrossing Networks. Please press...' Mason sighed and navigated her way through the 'voice jail' to a human operator.

'May I speak with John Woodhead's supervisor, please?' she asked pleasantly.

'Who may I say is calling?'

'Detective Inspector Mason. Staffordshire Police.'

There was an intake of breath at the other end. 'Please hold.'

About thirty seconds of Vivaldi, and a rather tremulous voice said 'Hello? James Birkett here.'

Mason introduced herself. 'You are John Woodhead's supervisor, I believe?'

'John works for me, yes.'

'And he went on a training course to the USA recently, I believe. Can you give me the dates, please?'

'Bear with me.' Mason could hear the sound of a keyboard at the other end.

'Wednesday of the second week in September to 20 December, just before Christmas. Can I ask why?'

'Sorry, I can't tell you that. I'd like to ask you a few questions about John Woodhead, if I may.'

'How do I know you are the police?' His tone was suspicious.

'Call me back on this number. It's the station switchboard. Ask them to put you through to me. Detective Inspector Jean Mason.'

'Will do.'

A couple of minutes later, her phone rang.

'James Birkett here.'

'Satisfied?'

'Yes. Please ask your questions. I've closed my office door, so if you need to know anything confidential, it will stay that way, at this end, at least.'

'Thank you. I'm recording this conversation, by the way.'

'So am I.'

She chuckled. 'Is John Woodhead in work today?'

'No, he hasn't been in for a few days now. He told us his girlfriend wasn't well, and he had to look after her. He's taking paid leave.'

Before she could stop herself, Mason reacted. 'That's a massive understatement by Mr Woodhead. His girlfriend was found murdered a couple of days ago.'

A loud gasp, then a few seconds of silence. 'That's terrible. Horrible. Why on earth wouldn't he—?'

'I don't know. Grief takes people in different ways.' *So does guilt*, she thought to herself.

'What...? Who...?'

'Exactly what I am trying to discover.' she said crisply, aware that she might have tipped her hand. 'Can we go on?'

'I suppose so.'

'Would you describe John Woodhead as a good employee?'

'He's extremely intelligent and quick on the uptake. That's why we sent him on a very expensive training course in the States.'

'There's a 'but' coming, isn't there?'

A sigh. 'Yes. He's very young for his age.'

'In what ways?'

'He can't stand being contradicted or criticised. I think there's a pressure cooker in there. Steam building up, and he's ready to explode.'

'Does he? Explode, I mean?'

'I've only seen it once. An expensive laptop found itself flying out of the window into the car park. He was warned that if anything like that ever happened again, he'd be out of the company within the hour.'

'Anything else?'

'Along with that, he is almost childishly pleased when things go right and he's praised. It's almost as if he's expecting sweeties for being a good boy.'

'But he didn't sound too emotional when he told you that he had to look after his girlfriend?'

'Upset, yes. Emotional, not really. Oh, Jesus Christ, this is horrible. Murdered? Can you tell me more?'

'Not really. Look in the *Express and Star* for the Stowe Pool murder.'

'Oh. That's her? Oh my God.'

'Afraid so. You have my number, Mr Birkett. Please call me if David Woodhead contacts you, or comes back to work.'

'I will. Goodbye, Inspector.'

❋

AT 2PM, Mason slipped out of the station and headed for The Boswell Bites café and a late lunch.

❋

Sunday 4 March 2018
Day 4 of the investigation

MASON CAME SLOWLY AWAKE to the ringing of her phone. Reaching over to the bedside table, she looked at the clock. 10.36. She picked up her phone. 'Mason,' she said and yawned.

'Kramer here, Boss. I'm at Dr Lunham's surgery. He's been murdered.'

'Bloody hell,' said Mason her mind instantly clear and alert. 'I'll be with you within 20 minutes.'

❋

THERE WERE THREE POLICE VEHICLES outside the clinic, one of them a van with FORENSICS on the side, a battered old Mondeo which she recognised as McGuire's, a Porsche, presumably the doctor's, and a small BMW hatchback. Whose? Mason had to do some clever manoeuvring to tuck her Picanto into a space.

After showing her ID and signing in, Mason put on a set of forensic coveralls and bootees, and ducking under the crime scene tapes, entered the clinic. She followed the steps into the reception area and through to the surgery. The doctor's body was on the floor in front of his desk, lying on his stomach. On the desk lay an open laptop, which one of the SOCOs had just finished examining and was putting in a plastic evidence bag.

'Morning, Jean,' said Dr McGuire. 'Do you realise that meeting the same woman three times in a week means marriage in some cultures?' he said with a smile.

'It's as I keep saying, Phillip, If only you were twenty years younger. What have you got for me?'

'Victim is Dr Gerald Lunham, aged 47, married. No children. This is what killed him,' said McGuire pointing to a two-inch hole in the back of the corpse's head. 'He was probably hit with the bust of Churchill that was lying beside him before Forensics snaffled it up. It had blood stains on its base and some skin and blood on the corner.'

'Could a woman have killed him?' asked Mason.

'Possibly, but I doubt it. You see, the assailant made doubly certain that he was dead by breaking his neck. There was no technique or skill to it – just brute force. Let's twist again like we did last summer.' He made a motion with his hands.

'Spare me the gallows humour, Phillip.'

'Whoever killed him really wanted him dead.'

'Who found him?' asked Mason.

'His wife. She's upstairs lying down. She says she came here and found him like this. I'll tell you something,' he grinned. 'You're going to get a surprise when you meet her.'

'Fine, have your little joke. I'll get out of your hair and let you get on.'

✳

LEAVING THE PATHOLOGIST and the SOCO team to their grisly job, Mason stepped outside and followed the stairs to the upper floor and the grieving widow. Mrs Lunham was indeed something of a surprise. Mason had expected a typical doctor's wife, well dressed, educated, middle-class, and middle-aged. Instead she found an woman who appeared to be Eastern European, taller than her by a couple of inches, and who looked to be no more than 25 years old, dressed like a stripper in a private men's club. Her long straight black hair hung over her shoulders and the dark makeup she had applied that morning was now streaked with tears, and a dewdrop hung from her nose.

'Mrs Lunham, I'm Detective Inspector Jean Mason. I know this must be difficult, but I have a few questions I must ask you.'

'If it will help catching the killer of my husband I will help.'

'When did you last see your husband?'

'This morning. Breakfast. Telephone call came and he said he had to see patient right then.'

'And what time was this?'

'Always he gets up early on Sunday to play golf. So before eight, I think.'

'Did he say who had called him?'

'No. He never spoke about patients to me. Said matters between him and patients were confidential.'

'Why are you here and not at your house?'

The other laughed without any humour. 'It is amusing. Or perhaps what I mean is that yes, it would be amusing if...' She stopped and sniffed.

'Go on.'

'Gerald had left the house without his lucky rabbit foot. See.' She held out a keyring with a rabbit's foot attached. 'Always he had it for playing golf. He said he never lost game when he had his rabbit foot with him.'

'And?'

'Yes, I decided to bring it to him here.'

'How did you get here?'

'That small black car. My car. It was gift from him to me. And I knocked on door, and no answer, and it seemed locked. So I went round back of house to small door that it is difficult to lock, and I knew that Gerald didn't always lock it. And it was open.'

'And then? I will ask you for a formal statement later, but for now please tell me.'

'I listened for voices, and heard nothing. Maybe patient has gone. Maybe Gerald has gone. But I opened door of room and saw... what you saw.'

'And then?'

'I became faint. I had to get away from that scene. I have seen death before, and I knew Gerald was dead. I knew there were beds upstairs for patients to rest. I came here to this bed and I called the 999 number. And then your people came.'

'I see.' Mason paused. 'Can I ask if you were you happily married? What I mean is ...'

'Were there other women? Was I expecting to catch my husband with other woman? Or man or boy?' She laughed mirthlessly. 'No. Gerald's weakness was gambling. It was his hobby.'

'Did he spend much on his hobby?'

'I think not. We were never short of money.'

'Thank you, Mrs Lunham. I'll arrange for a car to take you home and send an officer tomorrow to take a full statement.'

'Can they come please in morning? I have hair appointment in afternoon.'

'Yes. I'll send the officer in the morning,' said Mason with a straight face. Whatever tears Mrs Lunham had shed for her husband, her feelings were not going to delay getting her hair styled.

❃

RETURNING TO THE SURGERY, Mason was surprised to find that the pathologist and most of the Forensic team had cleared out. The only one left was a young man, whom Mason didn't know, examining the bookcase and its contents. 'You lot found anything interesting?' she asked.

'Yeah. There are several latent prints other than the doctor's on the bust of Churchill. One of them might belong to the killer. Or they might belong to the cleaning lady.'

'Is it all right if I have a dig around?'

'No problem, but can you keep it to the desk and the far wall, please?' I've checked all the books and journals in that bookcase.'

Mason started to examine the small bookcase which rested against the wall. Most of the books were medical along with a large range of medical journals including *The British Medical Journal*, *The New England Journal of Medicine* and *The American Journal of Medicine*. In addition there were folders containing articles on plastic surgery and abortions. Mason chose a 2001 copy of *The New England Journal of Medicine* to flick through. As she opened the volume the young SOCO shouted, 'Bloody hell.'

With a shaking hand, he showed Mason what he'd found. A book on plastic surgery had been hollowed out and resting in the middle of the pages was a computer stick.

Mason looked at the stick, her heart pounding in her ears. 'I'll stay here. Get your boss and the rest of the team in here. Every book and journal has to be examined. God knows what else is here.'

'Yes, Ma'am,' he said, running out of the room.

Two minutes later the Senior SOCO appeared at the doorway. He was white with embarrassment and two bright red spots glowed on his cheeks. 'My God, Inspector, I'm so sorry. I checked a few books at random and found nothing. That's why I gave it to Derek. I should have...'

'Don't worry about it. Can you examine this stick immediately and let me have details of whatever is on it by this afternoon and please check every book and journal in this room and any others you find on the premises. I'll get out of your way now. You can contact me back at the Station.'

'Yes, Ma'am.'

✳

THE CHIEF SUPERINTENDENT didn't like to be kept waiting, especially on a Sunday. For thirty years now he and his wife had always retired to their bedroom in the afternoon, talked out any problems they had and ended by having sex. And now it was nearly five and the unbroken run of 216 'discussions' was about to be broken. Without knocking, Mason entered the room.

'Sorry, Sir, but I now know it was Woodhouse who killed both Nicola and Dr Lunham.'

'So where is the little bugger?' asked Chief Superintendent Clarke.

Mason shrugged. 'West Midlands went round to his flat to pick him up. He wasn't there. Not at Nicola's flat, either. No sign of him or word from him. Parents haven't heard from him. Grandmother, who he's very close to, according to the family, hasn't seen him since Christmas. There's a cousin in Colchester who was very close to him when they were teenagers, apparently. Blank.'

'Put out a general call to pick him up if he's clocked?'

She nodded. 'Yes, but no press. Keep it among ourselves for now.'

Her mobile rang. 'Jean Mason. You what? You fucking what? I don't believe it. Well, yeah, actually, it's great news, believe me. Thank you.' She blew a kiss into the phone, and hung up.

'Go on,' invited Clarke.

'DNA messed up big-time. They told us the foetus had Damien Hunter as the father. Wrong sodding label on the wrong sodding test-tube or something. All a load of cock.'

'And that's good news?'

'It's bloody brilliant – the father, just as Nicola's dad told me, turns out to be David Wrekin. No more poisoned tree. I told him the truth to get him to confess and I didn't even know it. He was telling porkies about the vasectomy, or more likely he got a mate to do a cut-price job, and he made a balls-up of it.'

Clarke laughed out loud. 'That's funny. A balls-up on a cut-rate vasectomy. I like it. You should be on telly.'

'I'm happy doing what I'm doing, thank you, Sir. Anyway, that little shit's going down. Mind if I do a victory jig?'

'Be my guest. Well done.'

'Look, I'm certain that David Woodhead killed both Nicola and Dr Lunham. Maybe he didn't mean to kill her, but he did kill her.'

'You've got the doctor's statement,' objected Clarke. 'Saw him waiting outside the gate.'

'Saw someone waiting,' Mason corrected him. 'Description fits Woodhead. Fits several thousand others in Lichfield alone. Anyway, that doesn't let him off the hook. We don't know when she was killed. Some time between when she left the café when she was last seen alive, and seven the next morning when the body was discovered. The cold has really screwed things up with rigor and everything.'

'But you still think it's Woodhead?'

'Right.'

'Go on.'

'I got this just before I came to see you. It's the analysis of the doctor's phone come in from the HTCU. I haven't had time to look at it in detail, but there's a few interesting things that caught my eye. Just read the first paragraph of the report.'

Clarke took the paper and looked at it. 'I see. Accessing gambling sites thirty times a day or more.' He snorted. 'At least it's not kiddie porn.'

'Thank God.' Mason had been on a paedophile pornography case the previous year, and she had nearly resigned from the force as a result. Some things were too much to take. 'So let's say he was strapped for cash. He had to keep up that swanky house and that mail-order bride of his. And a Porsche. He had a nurse and a receptionist to pay. Even at the sort of fees he was charging, that gambling must have hurt him. I don't think he was the kind who'd be happy just putting a fiver each way on the 3:30 at Uttoxeter.'

'All right, so he was hurting. What has that got to do with the price of fish?'

'Listen. Go with me on this one, Sir. We know David Woodhead was unstable. Nicola's Dad told me. His boss at work told me. Just suppose Nicola told him that the child wasn't his, and it was David Wrekin's, and she was going to get rid of it?'

'He might freak out.'

'Right. Put his hands around her throat and tell her you're a slut, you're not going to do this. Whatever. And he kills her, not that he means to, but he does. Phillip McGuire found a bit of fingernail broken off in a scratch on her neck. Bet you that's Woodhead's.'

'Proves nothing even if it is. Could have been a bit of rough sex that morning. But it is circumstantial, I'll give you that.'

'And then he panics and starts shaking her. 'Come back, come back, oh God, I'm so sorry.''

'And bangs her head on the tarmac? Post mortem?'

'Right.'

Clarke thought about it for a moment. 'Yeah, it works. I can go with that. Especially now he's gone walkies. What about the dead doctor? Tell me what happened there.'

'This is partly guesswork, but it might make sense. Let's say that Lunham did see John Woodhead outside his drive that night. Except it was a bit after seven o'clock, and Woodhead was not alone. Lunham goes out to see where his patient has got to – maybe he thinks she's got lost and can't find his place – and he sees two figures struggling. Both go down, but only one gets up.'

'I'm with you. He wants money to keep quiet about the murder he's just witnessed?'

'Exactly, Sir. We know that Nicola was meant to be bringing £750 with her. I bet Lunham did a lot of his business on a cash basis – you can check with HMRC and the money boys.'

'And then he got greedy?'

'Right. And this is not guesswork. Look here.' She turned to another page of the phone analysis. 'This text here, sent the morning that Nicola's body was discovered.'

'"750 not enough. Another 2,500 by 9am Sunday. Same place as last time.' – whose number did this go to?'

'Woodhead's. They checked it out. And the irony of it is that we were doing the forensics around Stowe Pool when this was sent. Lunham could probably look out of his window and see us while he sent this.'

'So at nine this morning, Woodhead goes round to Lunham, with or without the two and a half grand—'

'My guess is without.'

'—and there's an argument, and Lunham gets banged over the head by Churchill and finished off with a broken neck for good measure. Very neat. But we ain't got Woodhead to tell us that you're right.'

'No but we will, Sir. He'll make a mistake and when he does we'll have him.'

'Find that little creep first. That's an order, Inspector.'

'Yes, Sir.'

❄

A FEW HOURS LATER, Clarke's phone rang again. He recognised Mason's mobile number.

'Yes, Inspector,' he sighed, annoyed at being interrupted once more on a Sunday.

'I thought you should know that the HTCU boys and girls have done a great job once again. The USB stick the SOCO team discovered?'

'Yes?'

'It's the doctor's unofficial account books. Cash payments from a wide variety of sources, stashed away in an offshore account on the Isle of Man. Many of the names are ones you and I might recognise. MPs, county councillors, company directors and the like.'

Clarke hadn't got to be Chief Superintendent by accident. 'Blackmail payments from the partners of the women on whom he performed abortions?'

'Yep, that's my feeling, Sir. It was enough money to feed his gambling habits and his lifestyle.'

Clarke considered this for a few minutes. 'Say nothing about this to anyone else, Inspector. That's an order. This is now my problem, and not yours. Send the HTCU report to me, and delete your copy from your computer. Understand?'

'Yes, Sir.'

❄

Monday 5 March 2018
Day 5 of the investigation

KEN JOHNSON, SERGEANT, Royal Marines (Rtd.) was up at 5.45am, made and ate his breakfast of bacon and egg, took a cup of tea to his wife of 43 years and at half past six exactly opened the back door to find Scamp, a cross between a Border Collie and Staffordshire Bull Terrier, waiting patiently. Slipping the lead on, he gave the dog a pat, said, 'Who's a good boy then?' and pulled the dog's ears. Despite the freezing cold, both of them were looking forward to a walk around Stowe Pool. There would be no-one about the ancient pool except the dog walkers, but he didn't mind. He'd been taking his dog for a walk around the pool every day for the last sixteen years, no matter what the weather was doing. The bloody police with their tent and tape had forced him to detour around the crime site and it hadn't impressed him.

When he arrived at the pool he was pleased to see that there was very little ice on the pool. 'Looks like you can have a paddle today, Scamp,' he said and undid the lead. Scamp scurried off to the edge of the pool and ran ahead to where the police tent had been for four days. The dog stopped and started to bark. Running into the water, he paddled out a couple of yards and grabbed a piece of cloth and started to swim to the shore. He was making very slow progress. Nearing the dog Johnson said, 'Drop it boy. It's just an old coat.'

But the dog kept pulling. Johnson walked gingerly down the embankment to the water's edge and said, 'Drop it ...' but never finished his command. Scamp had found an old jacket all right, but there was a pale white hand sticking out of the sleeve. Stepping into the freezing cold water, Johnson waded out up to his waist, grabbed the sleeve and pulled. He felt something give way underwater and the rest of the body floated to the top.

When he'd pulled it ashore he took out his mobile and dialled 999. Ten minutes later a bleary-eyed PC and a Sergeant pulled up on the road and jogged up the slope. Both were tired and the last thing they needed now was some geriatric old man thinking he'd found a body. One look and their attitude changed. They knew they had found John Woodhead.

Mason arrived at eight. The phone call had caught her in the shower, washing her hair. She immediately took a look at the body. It was most definitely Woodhead. Phillip McGuire was already on the scene, and had just finished going through the dead man's pockets and knew that his answer to Mason's first question would be a disappointment.

'Any suicide note?' she asked.

'Sorry, Jean, not a sign of one. The only things he had in his pockets are on the table. One leather wallet containing two credit cards, a membership card for a lap dancing club in Redwood City, California, £65 in notes, a couple of American $10 notes, a letter from Nicola to him dated last Monday, a penknife, loose change of £2.56, a phone, and a handkerchief. Also two phones, one of them pink with a girly sort of case, which might be Nicola's. There was also a half empty bottle of gin in the outer coat pocket.'

'No signs of injury on the body?'

'If you exclude what the fish have done, none. My guess is that he either lost his balance and fell in or he walked in. Half a bottle of gin inside him wouldn't help him keep his balance in any case.'

'A suicide?'

'On balance, and with no evidence to back it up, I'd say suicide. How's that going to affect your case?'

Mason smiled, 'For the best. I'm convinced that he killed both Nicola and Dr Lunham and there is a mass of circumstantial evidence to support that view, but nothing that a first year junior barrister couldn't destroy in 15 minutes.'

'I'll push Forensics to get back to you with their initial findings this afternoon.'

'Thanks, Phillip.'

❈

Mason returned to the station, and started to take down the 'murder wall' that she and her colleagues had spent the last four days compiling. She'd just finished labelling the box when the Super poked his head around the door.

'I hear you've found Woodhead dead?'

'Yes, Sir. There's no suicide note at the site and I doubt that I'll find one when I visit his flat later. If you want a guess, he knew he was going to get nicked, drank half a bottle of gin, went to revisit the scene of his crimes, and slipped, probably accidentally on purpose.'

'But he's our man?'

'Oh yes, Sir. He did it, I think we can say that. The phone records all point to that. But the truth is that without a signed confession we would have great difficulty proving it.'

'Never thought of looking in the pool, did you?'

'No, Sir.' She fell silent. 'But I did say we'd find her phone at the least if we drained the pool, didn't I? In hindsight, I suppose it was obvious where we'd find him, though. It all fits together, doesn't it? Like the last piece of a jigsaw.'

❈

The Lichfield Writers who contributed to this story:

Cathy Dobbs worked as a journalist for 20 years, with her last role being Features Writer at the *Express & Star*. She has lived in Lichfield for ten years with her husband, Nigel, and their son, William. Cathy has also sung with ther Codsall Singers for 14 years.

Diane Kenney, from a very young age, has always enjoyed writing but, due to work and family commitments, has never had the time to do more than 'jottings and scribbles'. Now, in a different stage of life she has the time to indulge and develop her creative writing skills purely for pleasure – at least for the moment.

Hugh Ashton has been a resident of Lichfield with his wife Yoshiko since 2016, having spent the previous 28 years in Japan. He has published several volumes of fiction, including the Sherlock Holmes adventure *The Lichfield Murder*.

Jim McGrath retired in 2012 to write full-time. He has published eight nonfiction books with Pearson Publishing, including the award-winning bestseller *The Little Book of Big Management Theories* and three police 'non-procedural novels' set in 1960s Birmingham.

Judy Boddington enjoys writing varied pieces of work, including creative pieces and poetry. She hasn't written creatively since leaving school but has written assignments for the Open University. She is now starting to look at her writing critically and is beginning to write in a variety of styles.

Pauline Moreland, born in Manchester, recalls writing her first "poem" at the age of six. Work demands took her to Canada, Israel, Italy, and France, before she settled in Staffordshire. Her more recent writing has been based on research for her MA in local history; poems only emerge during times of emotional stress!

Sientje Sherry moved to Lichfield in 1972, after growing up in Colchester, Essex. Lichfield is her home and she enjoys being in such a beautiful city – seeing the Cathedral and walking by Minster and Stowe Pools. But most of all she loves the friendly smiling people.

Sue Rusk is happily retired from a lifetime of working with young children in schools, nurseries and hospitals. Married with three grown-up children, two step-children and ten grandchildren under the age of seven, she enjoyed writing when younger, and is currently trying to fit it in again around school runs, babysitting and the continual demands of family life.

❋

The Lichfield Writers